High Mountains

Starlight Caves

Rainbow Pools

Huts

Ice Owls

Burning Bushes

Lake

Sledging Slopes

Gardens

School

Kennels

Ridge

Husky Training Ground

Fields

LAND OF ICE AND WINTER

Linda Chapman lives in Leicestershire with her family and two dogs. When she is not writing, she spends her time looking after her three children, reading, talking to people about writing, and horse riding whenever she can.

You can find out more about Linda on her websites at *lindachapman.co.uk* and *lindachapmanauthor.co.uk*

Books by Linda Chapman

BRIGHT LIGHTS

CENTRE STAGE

MY SECRET UNICORN series

NOT QUITE A MERMAID series

SKATING SCHOOL series

SKY HORSES series

STARDUST series

UNICORN SCHOOL series

Skating School

Sapphire Skate Fun

Linda Chapman

Illustrated by Nellie Ryan

PUFFIN

Madame Letsworth's Magic Ice-Skating Academy

ICE OWLS

ISSY   JO   MAISIE   MILLY

FROST FAIRIES

VANESSA   LOU   ABIGAIL   NARINDER

SNOW FOXES

NIAMH   JESSICA   CECILIA   SOPHY

To Charlotte Grant – number-one fan, eagle-eyed
reader and brilliant writer in the making!

PUFFIN BOOKS

Published by the Penguin Group
Penguin Books Ltd, 80 Strand, London WC2R ORL, England
Penguin Group (USA) Inc., 375 Hudson Street, New York, New York 10014, USA
Penguin Group (Canada), 90 Eglinton Avenue East, Suite 700, Toronto, Ontario, Canada M4P 2Y3
(a division of Pearson Penguin Canada Inc.)
Penguin Ireland, 25 St Stephen's Green, Dublin 2, Ireland (a division of Penguin Books Ltd)
Penguin Group (Australia), 250 Camberwell Road, Camberwell, Victoria 3124, Australia
(a division of Pearson Australia Group Pty Ltd)
Penguin Books India Pvt Ltd, 11 Community Centre, Panchsheel Park, New Delhi – 110 017, India
Penguin Group (NZ), 67 Apollo Drive, Rosedale, North Shore 0632, New Zealand
(a division of Pearson New Zealand Ltd)
Penguin Books (South Africa) (Pty) Ltd, 24 Sturdee Avenue, Rosebank,
Johannesburg 2196, South Africa

Penguin Books Ltd, Registered Offices: 80 Strand, London WC2R ORL, England

puffinbooks.com

First published 2010
1

Text copyright © Linda Chapman, 2010
Illustrations copyright © Nellie Ryan, 2010
All rights reserved

The moral right of the author and illustrator has been asserted

Set in 15/22 pt Bembo
Typeset by Palimpset Book Production Limited, Grangemouth, Stirlingshire
Made and printed in England by Clays Ltd, St Ives plc

British Library Cataloguing in Publication Data
A CIP catalogue record for this book is available from the British Library

ISBN: 978-0-141-33079-2

www.greenpenguin.co.uk

Penguin Books is committed to a sustainable future
for our business, our readers and our planet.
The book in your hands is made from paper
certified by the Forest Stewardship Council.

Contents

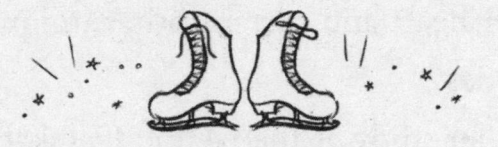

In the Magic Land of
Ice and Winter . . .

The weather was starting to warm up.
Every hundred years, the Dance of
Winter needed to be performed to keep
the magic land frozen and the snow thick
on the ground. Only an Ice Princess
could perform the dance, but choosing
an Ice Princess was never easy. She
couldn't be one of the ice sylphs who
lived in the land; she had to be a very

special human girl with ice-skating deep in her heart and certain other unique qualities.

In her study at the Magic Ice-skating Academy, Madame Letsworth, the headteacher, rested her chin on her steepled fingers and waited. Twelve human girls had been selected as possible Ice Princesses. Soon they would start to arrive. Would one of them be suitable? In six weeks, she would know the answer.

For now, all Madame Letsworth could do was wait . . .

Chapter One
Issy

Issy Roberts came bounding out of school, her blonde hair escaping from her ponytail, her bag thrown over her shoulder. Seeing her mum waiting in the playground, Issy waved, but before she could run over she was joined by Rosie, the girl who had been chosen to show her round that day.

'I'm really glad you've come to school

here, Issy.' The words came out of Rosie in a rush. 'Do you want to come to mine at the weekend? I could ask my mum.' Rosie blushed shyly as she waited for Issy's answer.

'Thanks.' Issy smiled at her. 'I'd like that. Bye, Rosie.'

'Hi, sweetheart,' Mrs Roberts said as Issy reached her. 'How was your first day?'

'Fine.' Issy flicked her thick hair off her face; her sideways fringe was always falling over her eyes. 'Everyone seems really fun.' Issy was used to starting at new schools. Her dad worked for a large company and they moved around a lot. Issy didn't really mind; she usually found making friends easy.

'That girl you were just talking to

looked nice,' her mum commented.

'Rosie? Yeah, she's asked me over at
the weekend.' At break time Rosie had
told Issy that her old best friend had
moved away a few months ago. Issy had
the feeling that Rosie would really like
her to be her new best friend.

But did she want to be? Something
inside Issy seemed to shrink away from

the idea. She'd had best friends before
and it was always really difficult when she
had to leave them. It was easier just to be
friends with everyone.

'Everything's all sorted out for your first
skating lesson tomorrow morning,' Mrs
Roberts said as they started walking home.

'Cool!' Skating was the thing Issy loved
most in the world. She'd done a lot of
gymnastics when she was little and had
been very good at it, but then two years
ago she had gone ice-skating and ever
since had thought about almost nothing
else. Issy loved whizzing around on the
ice. She wasn't quite as good as some girls
her age who had been skating since they
were three or four, but she'd been told she
had lots of talent and that she would soon
catch up if she kept practising.

'We'll have to think about getting you a new competition dress,' her mum went on. 'Your old green one is getting quite small.'

'I'd like a red dress this time,' Issy said, imagining herself jumping a triple loop in a sparkling red dress. 'Or maybe a dark-blue one with silver thread.'

They turned into the woods. There was a short cut there that led to the road where

they lived. Issy loved the woods. They felt
so magical and she liked the carpet of
spring flowers that covered the banks.

'Can I go and climb the oak tree?' It
was on the other side of one of the banks
that led down to the path.

'OK. I'll meet you at the end of the path.'

Issy ran up the bank, her school bag
on her back. There was a steep slope
running down the other side. As she ran
down it, she imagined she was skating.
Putting her arms out to the sides, she
leapt into the air, turning round as she
went. *If only I was on the ice*, she
thought, *I'd be spinning twice, feeling like I
was flying . . .*

And suddenly she was!

Issy gasped as she whirled round not
twice but over and over again. The

woods blurred around her, but before she had time to call out, or shout, she felt herself dropping down. Her feet touched the ground again with a bump.

In an instant, she knew that everything had changed. Freezing air stung her cheeks, her legs felt cold and her feet seemed heavy as if they had skates on. She looked down. 'Oh . . . oh, wow!' Issy gasped, almost falling over in shock. She was standing on a frozen river and she *did* have skates on!

Issy could hardly believe it. Her school uniform had disappeared and in its place she was wearing a dark-red jersey skating dress, matching wrap-around cardigan and white ice skates.

'Hello!'

Issy looked behind her and saw a large

stone mansion with turrets and a grand
staircase leading to the front door. A
woman wearing a blue woollen dress was
standing at the top of the stone steps.

'You must be Isabelle Roberts?'

'Y-yes,' Issy stammered. She stared at
the slim, dark-haired woman in
astonishment. 'Who are you?'

Chapter Two
Ice Owls

'I am Madame Li.' The woman came down the steps towards Issy. She had the largest, most pointed ears Issy had ever seen. 'This is the Ice-skating Academy in the Land of Ice and Winter. You have been brought here by magic. Come inside, my dear. There are eleven other girls here, so you won't be on your own.' The teacher handed Issy a pair of skate

guards to go over the blades of her skates.
'Madame Letsworth, the headteacher, is
about to explain it all to everyone.'

For the first time in her life, Issy felt
completely lost for words, but Madame
Li was waiting expectantly. Not knowing
what else to do, Issy slipped the guards
on and went up the steps into a large
hallway. A group of girls who all looked
about her age were just heading off down
a corridor.

'Take your skates off,' said Madame Li,
pointing out a locker to one side with
Issy's name on. 'You'll find some slipper-
boots in there. Put them on and hurry
after the others.'

Maybe it's a dream, Issy thought as she
dazedly unlaced her skates. But it didn't
feel like a dream. She could smell wood

smoke and the floor was hard beneath
her. Pulling on the fleecy red slipper-
boots that were in the locker, Issy
hurried after the other girls, catching up
with them just as they turned into a
grand hall. Twelve chairs faced a raised
platform where a teacher was standing.
She had pointed ears, just like Madame
Li.

Issy sat down at the end of the row.
The girl next to her was small with
glossy dark-brown hair. She had a
straight fringe, creamy skin and serious
hazel eyes. She looked at Issy and gave
her a quick smile. 'Hi, I'm Sophy,' she
whispered, but before Issy could answer
the teacher on the platform started to
speak.

'Welcome, all of you. My name is

Madame Letsworth. I am the headteacher here. I and all the other people who live here in the Land of Ice and Winter are ice sylphs.'

On the other side of Sophy, a tall girl with freckles put up her hand. 'But why are we here?'

'You were brought here because, every so often in this land, we have problems that can only be solved by a human girl

doing a magic ice dance. This girl is
called the Ice Princess. Sometimes the
Ice Princess helps us solve one type of
problem, sometimes another. We are
now in need of a new Ice Princess. We
hope one of you will be that girl.'

A murmur of excitement ran round
the room.

Madame Letsworth held up her hand
for silence. 'You do not have to stay here
if you do not want to; you may return
home. If you choose to stay then you
will live here at this school taking lessons
that will improve your skating. You will
also learn about this land. After six
weeks, we will choose one of you to be
our new Ice Princess. If that person
succeeds in helping us then she will be
granted her secret wish.'

She looked round. 'You must each now decide whether you will stay or return home. Do not worry about your friends and families; time passes differently in the human world from here and no one back in your world will even know you are gone.' Issy was glad about that. She had been worrying a bit about her mum, who was still in the woods.

Madame Letsworth looked round at the girls once more. 'Would anyone like to go home?'

None of the girls put up their hand. Quite a few of them, including Issy, shook their heads hard.

Madame Letsworth smiled. 'Excellent. Well, I hope you will all have a very enjoyable time here.'

Sophy put up her hand. 'What will the Ice Princess have to do, Madame?'

'She must perform the Dance of Winter – a special dance that needs to be skated every hundred years to keep this land frozen, but you will learn more about that in the following weeks. Right now, I am sure you would all like to see the dorms – the bedrooms where you will be sleeping. In the Ice Owls dorm will be Isabelle, Jo, Maisie and Milly.' Issy saw two girls with black hair and dark skin nudge each other as the headteacher spoke out the last two names. They were obviously twins although one had long hair in braids and the other had shoulder-length curls.

'In the Frost Fairies dorm will be Vanessa, Lou, Abigail and Narinder, and

in the Snow Foxes dorm will be Niamh, Jessica, Cecilia and Sophy.'

The tall girl with freckles leant forward. 'What's your name?' she said to Issy, and Issy told her.

'I'm Jo. We're in the same dorm. Isn't this all brilliant? We must do loads of fun things. Pillow fights!'

Issy grinned. 'Yeah. And a midnight feast!'

'And we have to play some tricks on the teachers.'

Just then, Madame Letsworth started speaking again. 'The frost fairies will now show you to your dorms, girls. They help do everything around the school; they tidy up, cook and clean. You'll soon get used to seeing them.'

The girls all gasped as a vast glittering cloud of fairies swept through the doorway. They were each just a few centimetres high and had masses of fluffy blonde hair. They chattered to each other in high-pitched voices.

One of them landed on Issy's hand, gauzy wings fluttering.

Jo pulled back as one approached her. 'Whoa! They're weird, aren't they? Like little wasps.'

Sophy, who had two of them perched on her shoulders, looked at her in astonishment. 'They're nothing like wasps! They're beautiful!'

Jo pulled Issy's arm. 'Come on! Let's go and find Maisie and Milly. I bet it's those two girls over there.'

Issy followed Jo over to where the twins were standing. 'Hi. I'm Jo and this is Issy. Are you Maisie and Milly?'

The two girls smiled. 'Yep, that's us. I'm Maisie,' said the twin with the shorter hair. 'And this is Milly.'

Issy immediately saw there were differences between the twins apart from their hair. Maisie's eyes were lighter and she had a restless, energetic look about her. Milly looked more serious and thoughtful.

Before they had a chance to talk any more, Madame Letsworth told the fairies to take them up to their dorms. The fairy who had landed on Issy's hand now perched on her shoulder as they went up the stairs.

'What's your name?' Issy asked her.

The fairy spoke in a high-pitched voice. It sounded like Cobweb.

'Cobweb?' Issy asked.

The fairy nodded.

'Well, hi, Cobweb. I'm Issy.'

The little fairy giggled as if to say she knew that already.

'Here we are!' said Jo as they reached a door that had a sign with the words *Ice Owls*.

'Cool!' said Maisie, going inside. The dorm had large windows looking out over the gardens. There were four single beds, each with a patchwork quilt. On the opposite side of the room there was a big wooden wardrobe for each girl. The frost fairies pulled the doors open. Inside there were plain skating dresses for wearing each day, outdoor clothes, lots of pairs of tights, underwear and socks, as well as other clothes like jeans and T-shirts. There was also a desk, some

shelves and a mirror on the inside of the
wardrobe door.

Maisie went over to the window. 'This
is so exciting!' She spun round, flinging
her arms out. '*I could have danced all night!*'
she trilled.

Milly looked up from the book she had
found on a bookcase behind the door.
'Don't mind Maisie. She's mad about
singing.'

'If I'm not a figure skater when I'm older then I want to be a singer,' Maisie said. 'I can't decide which would be more fun.'

'Do you two skate a lot?' asked Jo.

Maisie nodded. 'Every day.'

'I go skating three times a week,' said Jo. 'I've been skating since I was four.'

'I haven't been skating that long, but I love it and I go five times a week,' said Issy.

The frost fairies all flew to the door and chattered at the girls, beckoning with their hands. Issy frowned. 'I think they're telling us to follow them again. Are we about to go skating?' she guessed.

Cobweb gave Issy a thumbs up.

'Cool!' all four girls said at the same time. They looked at each other and giggled.

'You know, something tells me the four of us are going to get on really well,' said Jo, putting her arm through Issy's. 'Let's go and see the rink!'

Chapter Three
Skating at Last!

The ice rink was down a long corridor
and through some heavy double doors.
Issy looked round in amazement. It was
beautiful. Above the sparkling ice was a
domed glass ceiling through which they
could see the sky. Frost fairies darted
through the air and hovered round the
silver barriers at the edge. To one side of
the rink there was a large purple box

covered with silver buttons and nearby
was the changing area with wooden
benches and lockers.

The girls from the other dorms were
all arriving too. Sophy came in with a
very pretty girl with straight, shoulder-
length chestnut hair and a girl with wild
red curls.

The girl with the straight hair looked
worried. 'Oh, I wish you two had waited
a few more minutes so I could have
changed out of this dress. I look awful in
yellow. And I haven't even had time to
brush my hair.' She smoothed her hair
down anxiously. 'Do I look OK?'

'You look fine,' Sophy reassured her. 'I
like your yellow dress.'

'And I don't know why you're
worrying about your hair, Cecilia,' said

the Irish curly-haired girl. 'Look at mine.
My dad always says that it looks like I've
got birds nesting in it!'

Just then, Madame Letsworth came
through the doors. 'Your skates are in
your lockers, girls. You can go on to the
ice as soon as you like.'

Within five minutes, everyone had
changed into their skates. Issy skated
round the edge of the rink, moving from
one foot to the other, arms slightly out.
Some girls were going backwards, some
forwards; some were doing spins, while
others practised steps.

After a few warm-up laps, Issy began
to go faster and soon the urge to jump
overwhelmed her. Stepping back on to
the right outside edge of her skate, she
propelled herself upwards off her right

foot. Crossing her ankles, she spun round before landing on her left foot. A double toe loop! *Yes!* thought Issy as she glided round.

Speeding up again, she tried a double lutz. She fell over three times, but each time she just laughed and scrambled to her feet. Issy never minded how often she hit the ice. The feeling of getting a

jump right – spinning weightlessly and
landing perfectly – always made up for
it.

Issy finally landed the double lutz just
as Jo came over. 'Cool jump, Issy,' she
said admiringly and Issy glowed. 'Do you
want to play tag?'

'Yeah!'

'Got you!' said Jo, tagging her.

'Not for long!' Issy raced after her,
laughing as they dodged in and out of
the others.

After five minutes, Madame Letsworth
came on to the ice with Madame Li and
a tall male sylph with dark skin and hair.
She blew a whistle and gathered the girls
together. 'For your skating lessons you
will be taught in three groups. The
beginners will be taught by Monsieur

Carvallio, the intermediate group by Madame Li and the advanced group by myself.'

I'll probably be in the intermediate group, Issy decided. But a bit of her couldn't help hoping that she would be chosen for the advanced one. That would be so cool!

Madame Letsworth read out a list of names. 'In the beginners' group there will be Cecilia, Niamh and Abigail; in the intermediate group are Sophy, Vanessa . . .'

A girl with shoulder-length, dark-blonde hair gasped in indignation. 'But I *can't* be in the intermediate group! There must be some mistake. I'm an advanced skater!'

Madame Letsworth looked surprised.

'I'm sorry, Vanessa, but the teachers make the decisions about which group you will skate in.'

'I won't be in the intermediate! I won't!' Vanessa said, putting her hands on her hips.

'Who's a spoilt brat then?' Jo muttered to Issy, looking at Vanessa with dislike.

'Shh!' said Issy quickly.

Madame Letsworth's voice was firm.

'You will be in the group we have
chosen for you, Vanessa. If you do not
like it then you will have to return home.
Do you understand?'

Vanessa frowned. 'Yes,' she muttered
sulkily.

Madame Letsworth looked round. 'The
other intermediate skaters will be Lou,
Narinder and Jo; and the advanced group
will be Maisie, Milly, Issy and Jessica.'

Issy beamed. So she *was* in the
advanced group. Brilliant! She couldn't
wait for the lesson to start.

'There is one other thing I need to tell
you about,' Madame Letsworth
continued. 'At the end of each week
here there will be a competition. These
will help us decide who should be our
Ice Princess. The winner of each

competition will be awarded a pair of
jewelled skates.'

Jewelled skates! Issy swapped excited
looks with Jo.

'You will find out what the competition
will be tomorrow,' Madame Letsworth
continued. 'But we will expect you to
practise hard for it all week. You may
skate any time you like apart from when
you have other lessons to go to. Now let's
not waste any more time. Into your
groups, girls, and let's begin!'

Madame Letsworth spent ages working
through different exercises to improve
their footwork. Issy found that rather
boring. But she loved it when they got
on to doing jumps. She flung herself
around fearlessly and was delighted when

Madame Letsworth told her that she had
lots of ability. 'You just need to control
it, but well done, Issy. You've worked
hard today. I hope you'll get a lot out of
being here.'

Issy was sure she would! In the moments
she had been resting while Madame
Letsworth worked with someone else, she
had watched the other girls. They were all
very different, not just in how experienced
they were, but also in how they skated.
Maisie skated very dramatically whereas
Milly was more subdued, but very
graceful. Jo didn't seem to concentrate
much; she was naturally talented, but Issy
saw that she made quite a lot of mistakes
and didn't seem to really listen to her
teacher, Madame Li, when she was
corrected.

Sophy was the complete opposite. She couldn't do as much as some of the other skaters in the intermediate group, but she concentrated hard. By the end of the session, she was managing to do a double loop jump that she had been having problems with and Madame Li seemed very pleased with her.

And then there were the beginners. Cecilia had obviously not skated much

before, but, to Issy's surprise, once she stopped worrying about her outfit and hair, she seemed to have a lot of natural talent and she listened closely to what her teacher was saying. Niamh, the curly-haired Irish girl, who seemed to be always giggling and talking, was also a beginner. She was very flexible and fearless and Issy overheard her saying she did a lot of gymnastics at home.

There were so many different girls! Issy felt very excited at the thought of the next six weeks. What would they get up to and who would she be friends with? Most importantly of all, who would get to be the Ice Princess? *I hope it's me!* she thought.

Supper was in the hall. Frost fairies flew around, wings fluttering as they poured

out juice and brought plates to the table.
Issy wondered if she would see Cobweb,
but she wasn't there.

Issy, Jo, Milly and Maisie all sat
together as Ice Owls. Vanessa headed
over to their table.

'Oh, no,' Jo hissed.

'Hi, guys,' said Vanessa brightly as if
they were all the best of friends. 'Can I
sit with you?'

'Don't feel you have to,' muttered Jo.

Vanessa laughed as if she thought Jo
was joking.

'You three are all in the advanced
group, aren't you?' she said to the twins
and Issy. 'I should be too. Those ice
sylphs are completely mad. I've been
skating since I was three. My coach says
I'll be in the Olympics one day.'

Issy and the others exchanged looks.
Did Vanessa have any idea how boastful
she sounded?

'I have private lessons every day,'
Vanessa went on, sitting down. 'My dad's
a millionaire.' She looked around as if
expecting them to be impressed. 'We've
got a really big house – it's got ten
bedrooms.'

'Great,' muttered Jo.

Issy felt herself tense. Jo's sarcastic tone made her feel uncomfortable.

'We've got four cars and in my room I've got a TV and a PlayStation,' continued Vanessa.

Issy saw Jo start to open her mouth and chipped in instead. 'So, everyone, who's your favourite skater?'

'Sasha Cohen,' said Maisie immediately.

'Me too,' said Issy. 'Did you see her at the Olympics?'

'I actually *went* to the Olympics,' Vanessa said smugly. 'Mummy and I stayed at a five-star hotel, but we always stay in hotels like that.'

Jo looked at her with dislike. 'Do you think we care about your holidays and how big your house is?'

Vanessa looked taken aback.

'If you're going to sit with us, you'll have to shut up a bit,' Jo declared.

Vanessa scowled. 'Do you think I'd want to sit here if you're going to speak to me like that?' Picking up her tray, she marched off.

There was a moment's silence. Issy felt bad that Vanessa's feelings had been hurt. Milly looked a bit upset too, but Jo didn't.

'Thank goodness she's gone,' Jo said. '*Ooh, I'm going to be Olympic champion!*' She mimicked Vanessa's voice perfectly and Issy found herself smiling. Vanessa *had* been annoying!

'I'm very glad it's just us again,' said Maisie.

'Me too,' agreed Milly with relief.

★   ★   ★

41

After supper, they went up to their dorm and had a pillow fight. They shrieked and laughed as they thumped each other with the pillows. The frost fairies who were in the dorm, including Cobweb, perched on the curtain rail and watched, giggling.

At nine o'clock, Madame Li came round to tell them all to get ready for bed and then fifteen minutes later the lights were turned off.

'I hope we find out more tomorrow about the competition Madame Letsworth was talking about,' Maisie said as they snuggled down under their duvets.

'I love competitions,' said Jo.

'So do I,' said Maisie. 'I wonder what we'll have to do.'

Issy hugged herself. She couldn't wait
until the next morning to find out!

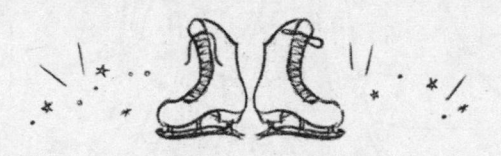

Chapter Four

Fairies and Dragons

When Issy woke up, the other girls were
still asleep. She was too excited to stay in
bed and so she went to have a shower.
When she came back, the other girls
were being woken up by frost fairies
tickling their faces with their wings.

'We're here! We're really here!' said
Maisie, sitting up and staring around.
'I thought it was just a dream!'

Cobweb flew round Issy's head, chattering. 'I wish I could understand you,' Issy said as the others started to get up and get dressed.

The fairy said something. Issy frowned. It sounded almost as if Cobweb had said, 'But you can!'

'Did you just say I *can* talk to you?'

Cobweb nodded and Issy definitely heard her speak this time. 'You just have to really want to understand. If you do and if you listen carefully then you will be able to hear what we're saying.'

'Oh, wow!' breathed Issy. 'Can I talk to all the fairies?'

Cobweb nodded again. 'If you want to.'

'What are you doing?' Jo said, looking at Issy.

'Talking to Cobweb! We can understand the fairies; we just have to really want to and to listen very carefully.'

Jo didn't look that impressed. 'But why would you want to talk to Cobweb?'

Issy stared. 'Because she's a fairy and it's fun! Have a go.'

Jo shook her head. 'Nah, not now. It's breakfast time.'

'Yeah, we should go downstairs,' said Maisie.

'Maybe later,' said Milly as Issy's face fell.

I guess they're just not into magic in the way I am, Issy thought in disappointment as she got dressed. For a moment, even though she was in the dorm with her three new friends, she felt rather lonely. *Oh, forget about it,* she told herself firmly. *It doesn't matter. So what, if they aren't interested in the fairies.*

Telling herself not to be so silly, she pulled on her tights.

The first lesson that day was about the Land of Ice and Winter. Their teacher was a grey-haired ice sylph called Madame Longley. She started off by telling them about some of the magical creatures who lived in the land. As Issy heard about ice monsters and snowball mice, icicle snakes and silver deer, she felt a longing to go out and explore. She couldn't wait to see all the creatures for real.

Halfway through the lesson, Madame Longley fetched a box from a walk-in cupboard in the classroom. 'We've done a lot of talking about magic creatures; now it's time for you to actually meet one. This is an ice dragon.' She took out a small pale-blue dragon about the size of her hand and there was a chorus of gasps. 'They live wild in the forests, but some of them also live in the school. They work the music boxes we have here. They are very friendly, but quite mischievous.'

As if to prove her point, the ice dragon

stuck out his tongue at the class. All the
girls giggled. 'You will see a purple
music box by the rink and there are also
boxes in the music room too. To make
them work you choose the type of music
you want from the buttons on the front
then the dragons inside will make the
music play.'

'How?' Issy asked.

Madame Longley smiled. 'With magic,

my dear. Now who would like to hold
Charlie?'

'He won't chip my nail polish, will he?'
Cecilia asked cautiously. 'It's such a pretty
colour.' She beamed proudly at her
hands.

'No, Cecilia, he will not.' Madame
Longley handed the dragon to Issy, who
had been the first to get her hand in the
air. Issy took the little dragon and cradled
him. He had long silvery eyelashes and
very dark eyes.

I'm holding a real live dragon, Issy
thought in wonder.

Charlie snorted out a cloud of
freezing-cold ice crystals.

'Bless you!' Issy said with a grin.

She wished she could hold him all day,
but the others were waiting. Issy

reluctantly passed him along to Jo.

Jo wrinkled her nose. 'Poo! He reeks. Smell that breath.' She passed the dragon quickly on to Sophy. 'Or rather, don't!' She grinned at Issy.

'Don't be horrid!' Sophy said indignantly. She glared at Jo and included Issy in the look. She held the dragon close to her chest and cuddled him. 'There, there,' she soothed him. 'You're

beautiful, aren't you? Ignore them!'

I didn't say anything horrid. I think he's beautiful too, Issy wanted to protest. Charlie rubbed his head against Sophy's finger. Sophy looked up at Madame Longley. 'I can't believe I'm really holding a dragon. Where do they live when they're in the wild?'

The teacher began to tell them all about ice dragons. Issy listened eagerly, but some of the others, like Jo and Maisie, seemed to get a bit bored.

Madame Longley put Charlie away and went to the board. 'Copy these facts out,' she told them, starting to write with her ice pen on the glittering white board.

'I know,' Jo hissed into Issy's ear, 'let's do the humming thing!'

She grinned and started to make a low

humming noise. She looked at Issy expectantly. Issy hesitated. She'd done this at some of the schools she'd been to – one after another everyone in the class started humming. It usually drove the teachers mad! But Issy didn't really want to do it now; this lesson was too interesting.

Maisie realized what Jo was doing and started to hum too.

'What's that noise?' Madame Longley said, looking round sharply. 'That's enough!'

They fell silent, but as she turned back to the board, Jo began to hum quietly again.

Sophy, who was sitting on her own in front of Jo, looked round. 'Shh!'

Jo shook her head. She nudged Issy,

her mischievous eyes urging her to join in. Issy didn't want to be a spoilsport. She sighed inwardly, but decided to start to hum too rather than fall out with Jo. Some of the others joined in as well.

Madame Longley spun round and pointed her ice pen at the ceiling. A shower of tiny hailstones pelted straight down at the girls! They all squeaked in shock as the freezing icy balls hit their faces, heads and arms, filling their laps, covering their notebooks.

'Finish!' snapped Madame Longley. The hailstones stopped. She put her hands on her hips and glared at the squealing girls until they fell silent.

'I told you that was enough.' The old ice sylph's voice was steely. 'Do you now understand?'

The girls all nodded quickly.

'Our books!' Jo said.

'Yes,' said Madame Longley. 'You will all
have to stay in at break time and copy out
your notes again. You'll find dry paper in
the cupboard.' Just then, the bell rang,
signalling the end of the lesson. Madame
Longley looked round at them and her
eyes twinkled suddenly. 'Enjoy your break.'

And, with that, she picked up the box

with Charlie in and walked out of the
room. There was a chorus of groans.

'Oh, great!' said Niamh, the Irish girl.
'Now we've got to write everything out
all over again.'

'And my hair's going to be frizzy,' said
Cecilia, taking a mirror out of her pocket
and smoothing down her hair.

'That was a really dumb thing to do,'
said Sophy, frowning at Jo. 'The lesson
was really interesting.'

Jo snorted. 'You must be weird to
think *that* was interesting.'

They glared at each other.

'Oh, come on,' said Issy quickly.
'There's no point arguing. Let's just get
on and write everything out again. I'll
get the paper.' She found a pile in the
cupboard and handed it out.

Sophy didn't say anything as Issy handed her a sheet. *It's not my fault*, Issy felt the urge to say to her as, grumbling and sighing, the class started to write the notes out again.

Chapter Five
Exciting News

Before they started their ice-skating
lesson after break, Madame Letsworth
got them all together.

'If you remember, I told you yesterday
that at the end of every week there will
be a competition. This week the
competition will be to make up a short
skating routine. You can choose your
own music and design your own

costumes – the frost fairies will make
them up for you. The winner will
receive a pair of sapphire skates. We also
have a tradition whereby the winner in
the first week is allowed to ask for one
thing. If the school can provide it then
she may have it.'

'We could ask for a midnight feast,' Jo
whispered to Issy, who nodded.

Sophy put up her hand. 'How will you
choose the winner, Madame?'

'We want to see you skating a
technically correct routine that tells us
something about you, a routine that lets
your personality shine through. It's
important that you realize this isn't about
how difficult your routine is. It's about
expressing yourself. Now go and get
your skates on ready for your lesson. The

teachers and I will be waiting on the ice.'

As soon as Madame Letsworth turned away, the noise level rose.

'We'll have to start planning what we're doing after lunch,' said Jo as she and the others hurried to the lockers.

'I might use a routine I've done for competitions before,' said Maisie, and Milly nodded.

Issy imagined herself flying around on

the ice, jumping high, spinning fast. She couldn't wait to start thinking up her routine!

Issy, Jo, Maisie and Milly ate lunch as quickly as they could and then went to the music room. The music boxes fascinated Issy. They had silver buttons down the front arranged in rows and columns. Every time the girls pressed a button, music flooded out. It was a bit like a strange CD player, but when Issy looked inside, she saw four ice dragons working a series of wheels and levers.

Issy couldn't seem to find a piece of music that she instantly liked, but she didn't want to spend ages choosing so in the end she picked a fast one that sounded OK. She would be able to do

lots of jumps to it. There were so many
things she wanted to put in – a double
lutz and a double flip, a layback spin, a
Flying Camel and some combination
jumps. The hard thing was working out
what *not* to include!

The others had all decided to adapt
routines they had used for competitions
at home and were spending ages trying
to find the right music. Issy decided to
leave them to it.

'Where are you going?' Jo asked.

Issy shrugged. 'Just to look around.'
But really she just wanted to talk again
to Cobweb, the magical frost fairy,
before lunch was over. 'I'll see you in a
bit.'

She left the music room and ran to the
dorm. Cobweb was there with the other

dorm fairies tidying up. 'Hi,' Issy said.

'Hello, Issy,' said Cobweb, flying to her shoulder. Issy frowned. Was it her imagination or was Cobweb moving more slowly than she usually did?

'Are you OK?' She glanced at the other fairies. Something wasn't right, she realized. It was taking three of them to move Jo's toothbrush from the desk back to the mug.

'We're not feeling very well today,' said Cobweb, following her gaze. 'It's such a warm day outside. When it heats up like this, we feel sick and our magic gets weaker. Magic in this land works best when the weather is very cold.'

One of the other fairies nodded. 'There are more and more warm days now because it's so long since the Dance

of Winter was last performed.'

'It's really hard to get all our work
done on days like this,' another panted.
She looked pale. 'It takes us ages.'

'You poor things.' Issy started tidying
up. 'Here, let me help. You shouldn't be
working if you feel sick.'

'No, don't worry . . .' the fairies started
to say, but Issy ignored them.

She hurried about the room, picking

up the last few things the fairies hadn't
got round to moving. 'It's fine. We
shouldn't have left our things in such a
mess anyway.'

Just then, the bell went. 'I'd better go
downstairs,' Issy told them. 'We've got
our first cross-country skiing lesson now.'

'Have fun!' called Cobweb. 'And
thanks, Issy.'

'Yes, thank you!' called the other
fairies.

Issy made her way to the back door,
where they had been told to meet
Madame Olsen. Issy had been really
looking forward to her first skiing lesson,
but as she went down the stairs, she
found that all she could think about was
what the fairies had just told her.

Jo, Maisie and Milly were waiting at the

back door with the others. 'Listen, you've got to hear about the frost fairies,' Issy said. Pulling them to one side, she told them what she had just learnt. 'I wish we could do something,' she said anxiously.

Milly nodded. 'That's awful.'

'I know,' Issy agreed. 'Maybe we could have a rota or something, to help them with the chores?'

'But I hate doing chores,' groaned Jo. She frowned. 'The frost fairies can't be that bad. The ice sylphs wouldn't let them work if they were really ill.' Maisie nodded in agreement.

Issy was disappointed that the others weren't more interested, but Jo was probably right about the ice sylphs making sure the fairies were OK.

Just then, Madame Olsen arrived and

clapped her hands. 'Right, girls! Let's find you some skis!'

Wearing skis felt strange at first, but Issy and the others were soon swishing across the snow in the woods, using their poles to help themselves along, and soon some of Issy's earlier worries fell away.

'I love skiing!' Issy declared at the end of the lesson, her eyes shining.

'Me too,' said Jo. 'We must come outside more. Did you see the slope in the garden? We could go sledging on that!'

'And we could have a snowball fight,' said Maisie, joining them.

As they headed back to the school, Issy's thoughts returned to the fairies. *Maybe all of us Ice Owls could try and think of something together*, she thought. *And then . . .*

She gasped as a snowball hit the back of her head. 'Jo!' she exclaimed, seeing Jo grinning at her from behind. Issy grabbed some snow and chucked it back, but unfortunately it sailed past Jo and hit Sophy, who was walking quietly on her own. Sophy gave a startled squawk.

Jo burst out laughing. 'Nice one, Issy!'

Sophy gave them a cross look.

'Sorry!' Issy gasped, but Sophy was already walking away and didn't hear.

Issy went to go after her, but was stopped in her tracks by a snowball from Maisie. 'Got you!' Maisie yelled.

Issy giggled and, forgetting about Sophy, grabbed some more snow and joined in the fight.

Chapter Six
Costume Crisis

The next few days flew by. Every free moment was spent getting ready for the competition. Issy changed her piece of music, but then, after a day, she decided she didn't like her new choice either. She picked another; it still wasn't quite right, but Issy decided it would have to do. Luckily she had always found it easy to think up and learn routines.

Issy couldn't wait to see her costume. She had designed a red dress with beading over the bodice and a floaty skirt. The frost fairies were making all the costumes and delivering them on the morning of the competition.

To Issy's relief, the weather had got a bit colder again and the frost fairies perked up, but Issy still made sure she did as much as she could to help them by keeping her things tidy and neat. Jo thought she was mad.

Issy sometimes had the lonely feeling she'd had on the first morning – she liked her new friends, but she didn't really feel they were very like her. Milly always had her head in a book and Maisie was always singing and messing around. Jo was good fun, but Issy had begun to notice that she just didn't seem to care much about people's feelings and she really wasn't into magic at all.

Issy wished there was someone she could talk to about Madame Longley's lessons and the frost fairies, but no one else seemed to feel the same as she did and so she kept quiet even though she was longing to talk about everything they were learning. *Jo, Maisie and Milly are great*, she reminded herself. *I'm lucky to have them as friends.*

On Saturday, Issy noticed that the frost fairies were behaving strangely. Groups of them kept gathering together, whispering anxiously. Issy wondered if it was because it had got warmer again that day. That afternoon, she found Cobweb

in the dorm struggling to pick up one of
Jo's socks.

'Here, let me do that,' said Issy quickly.

'Thanks,' said Cobweb, panting.

'Is the weather too warm for you
today?' Issy asked and Cobweb nodded.
'Is that why all the fairies look so
anxious? There are groups of them
everywhere.'

'We're all really worried about the

costumes for tomorrow,' Cobweb told
her. 'They're not finished because the
magic we need to make them has been
so weak recently. We're going to have to
stay up all night.'

'All night!' Issy echoed. 'You'll be
really tired. Can we help? Maybe we
could sew or something?'

'Thank you, but we do a lot of the
costume-making with magic. We're
going to try making the costumes down
by the ice rink because magic in this
land is stronger near to ice.' Cobweb saw
Issy's face. 'Don't worry, it'll be fine,
Issy.' She smiled, but it looked like an
effort.

The bell rang. 'I've got to go,' said Issy.
'But if you do think of a way I could
help, let me know.' She hated to think of

the fairies having to work through the
night to get the costumes done.

*If only there was something I could do to
help*, she mused. *But what?*

'You're being quiet,' Jo said as they
finished their supper. 'Are you still
thinking about those fairies?'

Issy nodded. She'd told them about the
costume problem as soon as she had sat
down.

'If I were you, I'd stop worrying about
it. There isn't anything you can do,' Jo
said. 'Look, it's still light outside. Why
don't we all go sledging?'

'Not me,' said Milly. 'I want to go and
practise my routine again and then finish
my book. I can't believe it's the
competition tomorrow.'

'You'll come, won't you, Maisie?' said Jo.

'Yeah,' replied Maisie. 'What about you, Issy?'

'I don't want to go sledging. I want to help the frost fairies.'

Jo rolled her eyes. 'Boring.'

'It's not!' Issy felt a faint flicker of anger. 'The frost fairies are going to have to stay up all night. They're weak . . .'

'Blah, blah, blah,' said Jo infuriatingly.

'Oh, stop being like that!' Issy exclaimed. 'It's really annoying.'

'Oooh,' mocked Jo.

Issy stood up. 'You don't care about anything, do you? All you ever want to do is have fun!'

'So?' Jo said with a grin. 'What's wrong with that?'

'Oh –!' Issy broke off with an angry exclamation. There was no point in arguing, but she was so cross. She pushed her chair back and walked away from the table. Sometimes she wondered why she was friends with Jo!

The dorm was empty. Issy lay down on the bed feeling miserable. If only she had someone she could talk to.

★　★　★

At quarter to nine, the others came back.
Issy felt strange after the argument, but Jo
didn't seem bothered. 'You should have
come sledging,' she said to Issy and Milly.
'It was fun.'

'It would have been more fun if there
had been more of us though,' Maisie
admitted. 'It's not so brilliant when it's
just two of you.'

Issy couldn't decide whether to still be
cross with Jo or not. She was glad when
the bell went a few minutes later and
Madame Li turned out the light. But
although the others fell asleep quickly,
Issy just couldn't. She lay awake, staring
at the ceiling, thinking about everything
– the fairies, her friends . . .

There must be something I can do . . .

Issy sat up. Oh, she couldn't just stay in

bed any longer. She would go and see them down at the rink. Pushing back the covers, she crept out of the dorm.

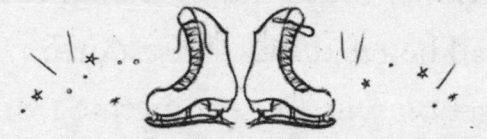

Chapter Seven
Skating Magic

Issy stole along the corridor. Just as she
reached the top of the stairs, she heard a
creak behind her. She swung round.
Sophy was coming down.

'What are you doing?' whispered Issy.

'What are *you* doing?' Sophy whispered
back.

Issy hesitated. 'Just something.'

'Me too.'

They stared warily at each other for a
moment and then Sophy shrugged as if
she had better things to do. 'OK, well,
you get on with your something and I'll
get on with mine.'

Issy followed Sophy down the stairs,
wondering where she was going. When
they reached the bottom, Issy expected
Sophy to turn off in the other direction,
but, to her surprise, Sophy went all the way
up to the double doors that led to the rink.

'Are you coming in here too?' Sophy
said, stopping and looking at Issy in
surprise. Issy nodded.

'Why?' Sophy demanded.

'I've come to see the frost fairies,' Issy
admitted. 'Their magic is weak because
it's getting warmer and they've been
having trouble making the costumes.

They've brought them to the rink because their magic will work best by the ice. I thought I'd see if I could help.'

Sophy's mouth had dropped open. 'But that's why *I'm* here. I'm friends with one of the fairies in my dorm. She's called Flaxie. She told me about the costumes tonight so I thought I would come along and help.'

Issy stared. 'You've worked out how to talk to one? So have I! I'm friends with Cobweb. I didn't think anyone else talked to the fairies.'

'I didn't tell anyone,' admitted Sophy. 'I didn't want the others to know. It felt really special that it was just me.'

'I tried to tell Jo and the twins how to do it, but they haven't even tried,' Issy told her. 'They're not into magic.'

'I am,' said Sophy.

They looked at each other and Issy felt
as if she was suddenly seeing Sophy with
new eyes. 'Let's go and see what we can
do,' she said eagerly.

They hurried through the doors.
Brightly coloured costumes were
hanging over the barriers. Some just
needed decorating; others had barely
even been started. Clouds of fairies
hovered over each one, some cutting,
some stitching seams; others in groups
were waving wands and magicking on
sequins and beads. A buzz of anxious,
high-pitched chatter filled the air as they
worked.

As Issy and Sophy walked in, two
fairies left the others and came flying
forward.

'Issy!'

'Sophy!'

'This is Flaxie,' Sophy said to Issy as a fairy in a pale-blue dress landed on her shoulder.

'And this is Cobweb,' said Issy, holding out her hand for Cobweb to stand on.

'What are you doing here?' Cobweb asked.

'We came to see if we could help,' said Issy. 'There must be something we can do.'

'Thank you for coming, but there really isn't,' Cobweb said.

But just then, one of the other fairies came flying over. She looked older and had a very wise face. 'There is actually something the girls can do that will help,' she said. 'They can skate.'

Issy, Sophy and the two younger fairies looked at her.

'Skate?' Sophy echoed.

The older fairy nodded. 'In this land, ice-skating creates magic,' she explained to the girls. 'If you were to dance on the ice then our magic would strengthen and we would be able to make the costumes much faster.'

'Well, we can do that!' said Issy,
glancing at Sophy, who nodded eagerly.

'We'd love to!'

The girls ran to their lockers and put
on their white skates. It felt strange to be
wearing skates with pyjamas, but as soon
as Issy stepped on to the ice, she forgot
about what she was wearing and just
thought about skating. 'We need some
music if we're going to dance,' she said to

Sophy. 'We could ask the dragons to play the music from our routines.' She skated over to the music box and looked inside. Four ice dragons were curled up on the floor, snoozing on little pillows.

'Um, excuse me,' Issy said softly. The dragons opened their eyes and yawned. 'We want to skate to help the fairies make the costumes. Would you mind playing us some music?'

The dragons sat up and made chirruping noises. Issy wished she could understand them as well as she could understand the fairies! But from the way they were nodding, she was sure they were agreeing.

One of the dragons flew out and pointed to the buttons as if telling her to choose.

Issy was about to push the button for the
music for her dance, but then she changed
her mind. The dragons never got to
choose the music they played. Maybe
they'd like to for a change. She could make
up a dance to anything and she didn't
really like her routine that much. 'Why
don't you play what you want?' she said to
him. 'It'll be more fun for you and I can
skate to anything if I listen to it once.'

The dragons looked surprised. The
one who was hovering by the buttons
flew up to Issy's face until he was level
with her nose. He stared into her eyes for
a long moment and then flew back into
the music box, chirruping and tweeting
at the others. They all nodded as if they
understood and began to turn the gears
and levers.

Issy didn't have a clue what all that had
been about, but the dragons looked
happy and music was starting to flood
out. Straight away it seemed to strike a
chord inside her. It was bright and lively,
but with a deeper undertone. It started
slowly and got faster and faster, building
up dramatically. Issy felt her feet start to
twitch. In her head she could already see
the moves she could do, imagine the
jumps and steps and turns. The music
reached its end and then the dragons
started playing it again from the
beginning.

Issy began to skate. She started slowly
with an expressive turn and then began
gliding from one foot to the other before
turning again and beginning some faster
crossover steps. She forgot everything,

thinking only about the music. As it got
faster, she took off into a double flip,
spinning over the ice. She landed the
jump perfectly and skated on before
turning into a fast upright spin, spinning
round on the spot on one foot, her arms
pulled into her chest.

More jumps followed – a double lutz
then a double toe loop – until the music
built to its climax. Putting her arms up

and arching back, Issy dipped into a
layback spin. Round and round she
went, holding her position as tightly as
possible, until she heard the final crash of
the music and she stopped, hands coming
down, head up, eyes shining.

'Oh, wow,' Sophy breathed, skating
over. 'That was brilliant, Issy!'

Issy was out of breath, but she didn't
care. 'It felt awesome! The music was
wonderful. I love it!'

'You should use it in the competition,'
said Sophy.

'I will,' Issy declared. The piece of
music was perfect for her. She wondered
if that was why the dragons had chosen
it.

'Look at the frost fairies,' Sophy said.
The ice dance seemed to have had a big

effect on them. They were now whizzing around, little sparks of magic jumping from their wands as they pointed them at the material. Sequins appeared instantly, beads attached themselves and dresses magically began to appear.

'Do your dance now!' urged Issy.

Sophy pressed the buttons for the piece of music she had chosen for the competition – it was a beautiful, lilting piece of music that made Issy think of a river running down a mountain. Sophy had chosen moves that were difficult, but she had clearly practised a lot and could do them all now. She was a beautiful skater to watch; every movement seemed to hold so much feeling. The only time she faltered was near the end, where Issy was expecting her to do a double jump and she didn't. She did a single flip before finishing her routine with a beautiful slow step sequence.

Issy clapped. 'That was great! Though you could have done a double jump instead of the single.'

'I know,' said Sophy. 'I was originally going to do a double flip, but I've fallen on it a few times when I've been practising . . . A single's safer.'

'But who wants to be safe?' said Issy. 'Don't be silly. I bet you can do it.'

Sophy looked uncertain.

'You can,' Issy urged her. 'Go on, try again. If you get it wrong, you get it wrong. But it's better to try.' She skated to the music box and asked the dragons to play the music again. 'Just go for it!'

And Sophy did. She skated the rest of

the dance as perfectly as she had the first time and then, as she reached the final part of the routine, she threw herself into the jump, turning round twice in the air. She landed it with just the smallest wobble. Issy cheered.

There was the sound of clapping from the frost fairies. Sophy finished the routine with her step sequence and then looked round as Cobweb and Flaxie

came flying over. 'That was a great jump,
Sophy!' Flaxie said.

Sophy looked very pleased. 'Thanks.'
She glanced at Issy. 'I'll definitely keep it
in. How are the costumes going?' she
asked the fairies.

'Much better. Your dancing is really
helping. Can you carry on?'

Issy and Sophy grinned at each other.
'Of course we can!'

The girls skated for an hour more, taking
it in turns and then teaching each other
their dances. By the end of it, the frost
fairies had finished the costumes! 'All
we've got to do is deliver them to the
dorms!' said Cobweb in delight.

'And then we can go to bed,' said
Flaxie.

The older fairy flew over. 'Thank you so much, girls,' she said to Issy and Sophy. 'Without your help we'd have been working all night.'

'I don't understand why you didn't just ask people to come and skate,' said Issy. 'Everyone would have wanted to help get their dress finished and, besides, we all love skating!'

'Ah, but the magic wouldn't have worked then. It only worked because you *wanted* to help us — and not just because we asked you to. That's the way it is in this land.' The fairy smiled at them. 'You'll find out more about that in time.'

'You mean, when we find out more about the Ice Princess?' said Sophy eagerly.

'Yes. Now go and get some sleep. You have a competition tomorrow!'

Issy and Sophy went up the stairs together, the frost fairies flying ahead of them with the glittering costumes. The girls stopped as they reached the landing. 'It's been really fun tonight,' Issy said.

'Yeah,' Sophy agreed, her eyes warm and friendly. 'You're not at all like I thought you were.'

'What do you mean?' Issy asked.

'Well, I thought you didn't care about magic.'

'But I do!'

'I know that now.' Sophy looked at her curiously. 'So why do you mess around so much in lessons?'

'I don't really – it's Jo who does,' said Issy. 'She's not into magic.'

'I don't get why you're friends with her,' Sophy said.

'She's nice,' Issy said loyally. 'And fun.'
She didn't add *even though she can be a
bit annoying at times* because she never
liked it when people were mean about
their friends behind their backs. 'I do
like her, but she *is* different from me.'
She went on quickly, 'It's so silly. I've
been wishing there was someone here
who liked magic, who I could be
friends with, and I didn't think of you.
You just seemed really quiet and
serious.'

'I guess we both got it wrong,' said
Sophy.

Issy hesitated. 'Can we be friends
now?' she blurted out hopefully.

Sophy smiled. 'Definitely.'

Issy felt very happy. 'Cool! I'll see you
tomorrow then.'

Sophy nodded. 'All ready for the competition.'

Excitement rushed through Issy. Now she had some music she liked, she couldn't wait!

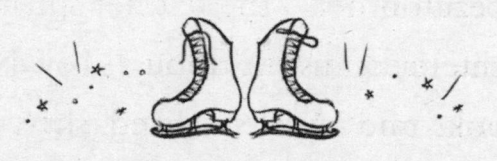

Chapter Eight
Competition Day!

'Wake up!' Issy felt someone shaking her shoulder. She opened her eyes and saw Jo leaning over her. 'Our costumes are here!'

Issy sat up, yawning. She felt worn out after the night before, but as it all came flooding back and she remembered what had happened – how she and Sophy had helped the frost

fairies and how they had made friends
with each other – she felt her spirits lift
and the tiredness slip away.

'Look!' said Maisie, waving a silver
skating dress under her nose.

'This is yours,' said Milly, holding up a
red dress for Issy to see.

'I know.' Issy took the beautiful deep-
red dress with the chiffon skirt. 'I saw it
last night.'

'Last night?' Jo echoed in surprise.
'What do you mean?'

Issy told them what had happened —
everything apart from her conversation
with Sophy on the staircase. She kept that
to herself. She wasn't sure how Jo would
feel about her being friends with Sophy.

Looking at Jo now, she wondered how
she felt about her. Should she be in a
mood with her still? *No*, Issy decided.
Her time here was too short to fall out
with people. And even though Jo could
be annoying, they shared a dorm and she
was fun to be around. *And I've got Sophy
now as well*, Issy realized. A warm glow
spread through her at the thought.

The others were astonished to hear
about the night before. 'Why didn't you
wake us up?' demanded Jo.

'It just kind of happened,' said Issy.

'It's brilliant you helped,' said Milly.

'And that all our costumes are ready,' said Maisie, starting to try hers on. 'I can't wait to skate in mine!'

The morning was free for the girls to practise for the competition. When Issy got to the rink in her costume, she saw Sophy there, getting her skates out of her locker. For a moment, Issy felt almost shy, but then Sophy turned and saw her and a smile lit up her face.

Issy ran over. 'Hi! Last night was cool, wasn't it?'

'Very,' agreed Sophy.

'Your dress looks lovely,' Issy said. Sophy was wearing a blue velvet dress with silver sequins on the bodice.

'So does yours.' Sophy smiled. 'Shall
we warm up together?'

'Definitely!' As Issy got her skates out,
she felt like singing. She had the feeling
that for the first time in ages she might
have made a really special friend. *A best
friend*, she thought and suddenly it
seemed like a very good thing after all.

Issy practised all morning. The happiness
inside her made her feel as if she was
sparkling when she was skating, and now
she had the right music, Issy knew she
had a great routine.

After lunch, the girls did their hair.
They were also allowed to wear make-up
for the competition. Issy put on some
glittering silver eyeshadow and mascara
to darken her eyelashes. Then she added

a bit of lipgloss and a dusting of glitter across her cheekbones. Her hair was pulled back in a bun and she wore sparkling silver clips in it. Finally she changed into her red dress and tan tights.

Issy looked in the mirror and smoothed down the floaty skirt. This was it! She took a deep breath. The competition was about to begin!

The three skating teachers were the judges and they sat behind a big table. Other ice sylphs filled the seats round the rink. After each girl had skated and been given a mark, the frost fairies flew up and formed the mark in the air. As Issy waited for her turn, she felt nerves and excitement racing through her.

She paced around as she watched

Milly's slow, elegant routine and Maisie's lively, theatrical one. She saw Jo making some mistakes in hers, but laughing them off. Curly-haired Niamh raced around and fell over three times, but jumped up every time and just carried on, not caring. Vanessa skated in a very show-offy way, but without really being in time to the music.

Finally it was Sophy's turn. She skated

her routine beautifully, moving perfectly with the music, her hands and arms held in a lovely line, all her moves full of expression and feeling. When she got near the end, Issy held her breath and then burst into applause as Sophy managed to jump the double flip. She'd done it perfectly!

'Well done!' cried Issy as Sophy finished and came off the ice, her eyes shining.

'That was brilliant, Sophy,' said Niamh. 'And look!' she said as the frost fairies showed Sophy's mark. 'You're in the lead!'

And then it was Issy's turn. She felt the nerves pounding through her, but as she stepped on to the ice, her worries faded away. This was where she belonged. She stood in the centre of the ice feeling calm but excited as she waited for her music to start. *You can do it!* she told herself. *You really can!*

The first few notes echoed out and Issy was off. She didn't think about the audience or the fact that this was a competition. All she thought about was skating. She threw herself into all her jumps with every ounce of energy in her body.

On her final combination, Issy was so carried away she tried to turn a triple toe loop instead of a double toe loop. She didn't quite manage it. As she stumbled on the landing and almost fell, she realized she might have just lost her chance of winning, but she didn't care. She skated on and, as the music neared the end, dipped

into her layback spin, her eyes up towards
the domed glass ceiling, her arms above
her, fingers touching, back arched. She
spun around faster and faster until she
stopped exactly on the last beat.

Everyone burst into applause. Panting
and smiling, Issy skated off the ice. She
might have fluffed the triple toe loop,
but it had felt right to try it and she was
glad she had.

As she came off the ice, Sophy hugged her and Issy's marks went up. She was in third place, with Sophy first and Maisie second. That was the way the marks stayed when Jessica, the final skater, came off the ice.

'You did it! You won, Sophy!' Issy gasped. Sophy was open-mouthed in shock.

'I can't believe it!'

Niamh came over and hugged her. 'Well done!' The other girls started crowding around and congratulating her.

Madame Letsworth stood up and called for silence. 'Well done, girls!' she said as the girls and audience quietened down. 'You should all be very proud of yourselves. You have all skated very well indeed. The marks were awarded for two things — accuracy and style — but we were looking particularly at how well we felt you expressed yourself on the ice. Our winner this week is Sophy, who skated a beautiful routine full of personality with very few faults. Sophy, would you like to come and collect the sapphire skates?'

Sophy skated on to the ice to the sound of clapping and cheers. Madame Letsworth handed her a beautiful pair of skates, decorated with sparkling blue sapphires. 'Well done,' she said, smiling at Sophy. 'You have worked very hard this week and thoroughly deserve to win. Now, as part of your prize, you are allowed to ask the school for something. What will it be?'

Sophy thought for a moment. 'Can we

have a sledging party?' she asked. 'For
everyone this afternoon?'

'Of course!' Madame Letsworth smiled
and all the girls cheered in delight. 'Go
and get changed now, girls. You have
worked very hard and now it is time for
you to relax and have some fun!'

Half an hour later, the school gardens
were ringing with the sound of shouts

and laughter as the girls pulled sledges up the hill in the garden and then tobogganed down.

Every girl was there. As Issy pulled the sledge up to the top of the hill with Sophy, she looked round. Milly was sitting on her sledge reading a book. Niamh was giggling and trying to stand up on the sledge as if it was a surfboard. Cecilia was looking in a pocket mirror and checking her bobble hat was straight, while Jo and Maisie were whooshing down the slope, wicked grins on their faces as they passed a few centimetres away from where Vanessa was standing sourly, sending a wave of snow crystals flying all over her and making her yell.

'I can't believe we've only been here

for six days,' Issy said to Sophy. It felt like she'd known everyone forever.

'I'm really glad last night happened. I can't believe we were stupid enough not to make friends until then,' Sophy told her.

'We'll make up for it now.' Issy hoped Jo would be OK with that. She had looked a bit put out when Issy had said she was going to go on Sophy's sledge.

'Do you think we'll find out more about the Ice Princess next week?' said Sophy as they reached the top and got the sledge into position. 'I want to know more about the dance she has to do and how they're going to choose her.'

'Me too. Maybe it'll be you, seeing as you won the competition,' said Issy.

'But there are five more competitions to go,' Sophy pointed out as they got on

to the sledge together. 'I hope next
week's will be fun too.'

Issy grinned. 'I bet it will be!' She
wrapped her arms tightly round Sophy's
waist. 'OK, are you ready?'

'Yep!' Sophy called.

Issy grinned. 'Then here we go!' She
pushed off as hard as she could and they
shot down the slope, their shrieks of
laughter echoing up into the pale-blue sky.

Do you dream of becoming an Ice Princess?

Have you ever wanted to go to a REAL Skating School?

All readers of *Skating School* get FREE membership to the National Ice Skating Association's Skate UK programme!

Skate UK will help you to learn all the moves and basic skills you need to become a true Ice Princess! It's all about fun and continuous movement and is taught in groups, so why not share your love of *Skating School* with your friends and bring them too?

To get your free membership, go to
www.iceskating.org.uk/skatingschool
and enter the secret password: **Twirl**.

Skate UK is taught by licensed NISA coaches and can be assisted by trained Programme Assistants.

For full terms and conditions visit:
www.lindachapman.co.uk
www.iceskating.org.uk/skatingschool

Do you want to enter super competitions, get sneak previews and download lots of *Skating School* fun?

Get YOUR skates on
join the
Sparkle Club
today!
lindachapman.co.uk

Just enter this secret password:

Twirl

The Land of Ice and Winter is waiting for you ...

Design your own ice-skating dress!

The tiny frost fairies have been working overtime designing the beautiful dresses for the girls to wear in the Ice-skating Academy competitions.

Using this dress as a template, the fairies need you to draw the most magical ice-skating outfit you can think of. Every month one lucky winner will receive a magical *Skating School* goody bag!

Send your drawing

with your name and address to:

Skating School Competition, Puffin Marketing, 80 Strand, London WC2R 0RL

Or e-mail them to: **skatingschool@uk.penguingroup.com**

Welcome to the magical Land of Ice and Winter

… a world where all your dreams come true!

Join in the magic with Emily and her friends in the very first *Skating School* series

Hi there,

I hope you've enjoyed reading about the adventures of the girls who go to the Magic Ice-skating Academy. I love writing them all down! Wouldn't it be amazing to go to the Land of Ice and Winter and see all the creatures who live there? Can you imagine holding an actual ice dragon or talking to a frost fairy?

Sometimes readers write to me and ask about my life. Being a writer is the best job ever. I live in a cottage in a village with my family and two dogs – a Bernese mountain dog and a golden retriever. I spend my days writing and going to visit schools and libraries to talk about writing.

I always think I'm really lucky because I get to spend my days writing about magic – mermaids, unicorns, stardust spirits, genies and now the Land of Ice and Winter. If you love them too then why not go to **www.lindachapman.co.uk** and join the Sparkle Club? It's my online fan club with loads of activities and downloads, and you can only get to it by using the secret password at the back of this book. Have fun!

Love,

Linda
xxx